For Rilynne

A thank-you song to Christy Ottaviano
to be sung to a tune by The Commodores:

She should change her name to OTTER-viano.

(Chorus)
She's a WORD—HOUSE!
Re-write, re-write me, she takes all my bad words out.
She's a WORD—HOUSE!
Her brain is stacked with lots of facts.
She's nice and she has no plaque.

(Bridge)
She knows nouns, she knows nouns, she knows nouns now. *(Repeat)*

* * *

Thanks, Mom, Scott, and Joan, for your
continuous support and encouragement.

H SQUARE FISH

Imprints of Macmillan Publishing Group, LLC
120 Broadway, New York, NY 10271
mackids.com

Square Fish books may be purchased for business or promotional use. For information on bulk purchases, please contact the Macmillan Corporate and Premium Sales Department at (800) 221-7945 x5442 or by e-mail at specialmarkets@macmillan.com.

Library of Congress Cataloging-in-Publication Data
Keller, Laurie.
Do unto otters: a book about manners / Laurie Keller.
p.   cm.
Summary: Mr. Rabbit wonders if he will be able to get along with his new neighbors, who are otters, until he is reminded of the golden rule.
[Golden rule–Fiction. 2. Neighborliness–Fiction.
3. Rabbits–Fiction. 4. Otters–Fiction.] I. Title.
PZ7.K281346Do 2007   [E]–dc22   2006030505

Originally published in the United States by Christy Ottaviano Books, an imprint of Henry Holt and Company
First Square Fish Edition: 2009
Square Fish logo designed by Filomena Tuosto

ISBN 978-0-8050-7996-8 (Henry Holt hardcover)
30 29 28 27 26 25 24 23 22 21

ISBN 978-0-312-58140-4 (Square Fish paperback)
20

F&P: M / LEXILE: AD460L

This book is based on the Golden Rule.

Otts and Ends

Hi, Hilde!

Do Unto Otters

(A Book About Manners)

By

Laurie Keller

Doo-
Dee-
Doo

EXTRA TWIGS

She could've drawn LESS HEAVY boxes!

ROCKS

THIS END UP

SQUARE FISH

Henry Holt and Company
New York

Hello, Mr. Rabbit.
We're your new neighbors,
the OTTERS!

I don't know anything about <u>otters</u>.

What if we don't get along?

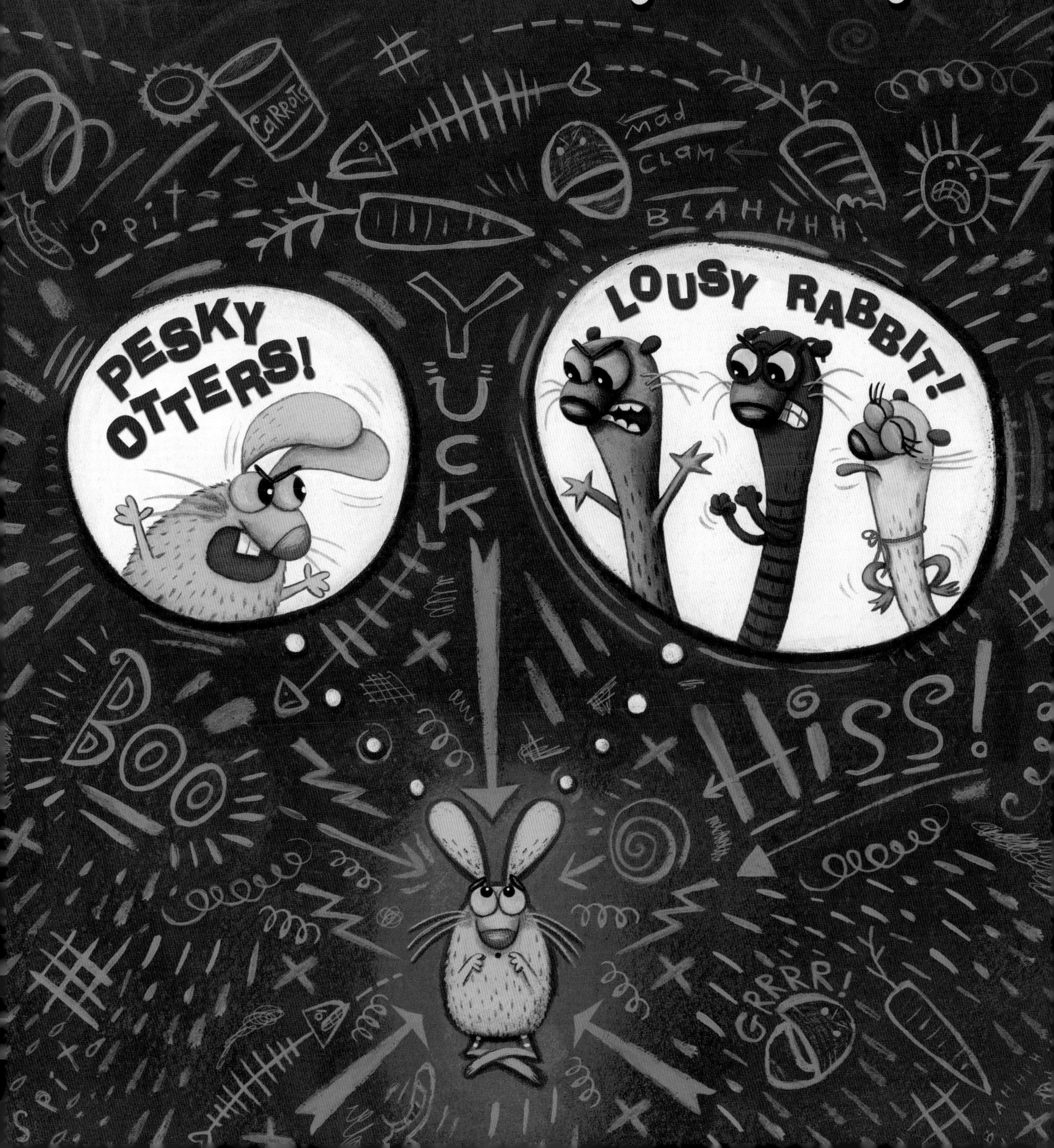

Mr. Rabbit, I know an old saying:

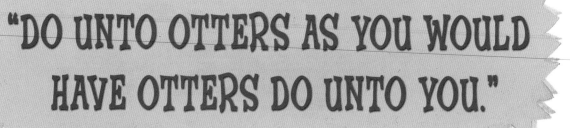

"DO UNTO OTTERS AS YOU WOULD HAVE OTTERS DO UNTO YOU."

What does **THAT** mean?

It simply means treat otters the same way you'd like otters to treat you.

Treat otters the same way I'd like otters to treat me?

Hmmm...

How would I like otters to treat me?

How would I ....

...like OTTERS...

...to treat ME?

Well . . . I'd like otters to be FRIENDLY.

A cheerful hello,

a nice smile,

and good eye contact

are all part of being friendly.

Friendliness is very important to me—especially after my last neighbor, Mrs. Grrrrrrr.

I'd like otters to be POLITE.

They should know when to say

"PLEASE."

PLEASE LOOK

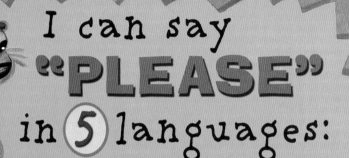

They should know when to say

"THANK YOU."

THANKS FOR LOOKING! C:

Would you like me to sting you now?

NO, thank you.

Then please take my BEE-zness card and call me when you're ready.

Dear Mr. Rabbit,
Thank you very much for returning my ball. You must have returned a lot of balls before because you made it look so easy! Balls sure are bouncy (and roll-y) but I'll try to keep it under control next time.
Sincerely,

Nice beak.

Thanks!

I can say "THANK YOU" in 5 languages:

"Gracias" (Spanish)

"Merci" (French)

"Danke schön" (German)

"Arigato" (Japanese)

"Ankthay ouyay" (Pig Latin)

Superb!

Did you say "PLEASE" or "CHEESE"?

And they should know when to say

"EXCUSE ME."

EXCUSE ME!
BURP

EXCUSE ME!!!

Oh, Ms. Otter!

Excuse me, Mr. Bee, I need to run and check on something...

OOPS!

I can say "EXCUSE ME" in ⑤ languages:

"Dispénseme" (Spanish)

"Pardonnez-moi" (French)

"Entschuldigen Sie" (German)

"Sumimasen" (Japanese)

"Excuseway emay" (Pig Latin)

Well, "P-U" is the same in ANY language!

Pffft!

Hmm . . . it worked in rehearsal.

Excuse me for interrupting your reading, but I heard you say "PLEASE," not "CHEESE!"

Otters should be

HONEST.

That means they should

KEEP THEIR PROMISES

My word is as good as GOLD (fish)!

NOT LIE

I never lie— it makes my whiskers itch.

NOT CHEAT

Cheating makes my whiskers itch, too. . . . I wonder if I should see a doctor?

I'd like otters to be CONSIDERATE.

You know...

BEING A GOOD LISTENER

ASKING BEFORE BORROWING SOMETHING

NOT LITTERING

BEING PATIENT

CARING FOR ALL CREATURES (big and small)

OPENING THE DOOR FOR SOMEONE

BEING ON TIME

RESPECTING THE ELDERLY

HELPING NEIGHBOR UNTANGLE EARS

It's always good to have a considerate neighbor.

It wouldn't hurt otters to be KIND.

(Everyone appreciates a kind act
no matter how bad it smells.)

I see otters
like to play.

Wheeeeeee!

I'd like it if we could SHARE things:

our favorite books,

Harry Otter

Goldilocks and the Three Hares

our favorite activities,

our favorite treats

(hmmm . . . maybe not the treats).

I hope otters **WON'T TEASE** me about:

My "Doo-Dee-Doo" song

My extra-large swim fins

My "bad hare days"

I think otters should **APOLOGIZE** when they do something wrong.

And I hope they can be FORGIVING when I do something wrong.

So there.
That's how I'd
like otters to
treat me.

You see,
Mr. Rabbit,
I told you it
was simple!

RIGHT! Just
"DOO-DEE-DOO
unto otters as you
would have otters
DOO-DEE-DOO
unto you!"